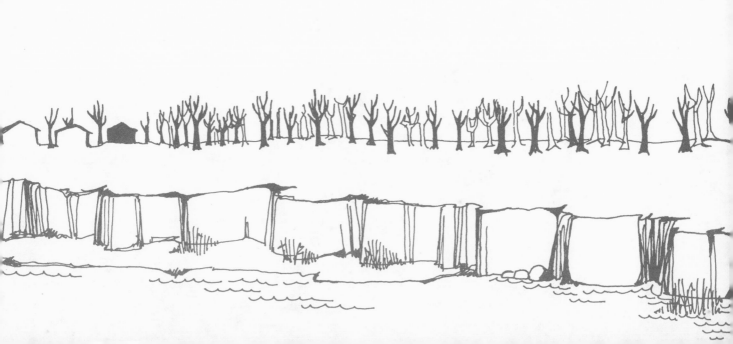

A Child's Christmas
in Memphis
1833

Great Corn Moon
(Sept.) 1983

RISING FAWN AND THE FIRE MYSTERY

For Ruth and Jim –
friends and neighbors –
"Be still ..."
Love, Marilou/Lulu/Awiakta

"..... and listen"
Beverly Bringle

Roger R. Easson, Series Editor

A Child's Christmas in Memphis, 1833

RISING FAWN AND THE FIRE MYSTERY

Told by
Marilou Awiakta

Drawn by
Beverly Bringle

St. Luke's Press
1983

Library of Congress Cataloging in Publication Data

Awiakta, Marilou, 1936–
    Rising Fawn and the fire mystery.

    Summary: Rising Fawn, a young Choctaw girl preparing to leave Mississippi with her family to travel west to a reservation, is kidnapped and subjected to an entirely different destiny.
    [1. Choctaw Indians—Fiction. 2. Indians of North America—Fiction. 3. Kidnapping Fiction]
I. Title.
PZ7.A9615Ri   1983   [Fic]   83-13824
ISBN 0-918518-29-6 (pbk.)

MY THANKS TO THOSE WHO HELPED ME

When in December, 1982, Irving Knight said, "I want to tell you about my great-grandmother . . ." that was the beginning of this story. The rest of it fell into place later when Beverly Bringle told me of the account of her great-grandfather, Tushpa, written by his son, James Culberson. I am indebted to Ruth Culberson Robertson of Oklahoma for releasing her father's treasured manuscript to my care. And this story could not have been written without the Choctaw themselves, who have been very generous in sharing their heritage with me. I am especially grateful to William Brescia, Director of Research and Curriculum Development, Mississippi Band of Choctaw Indians; Grady John of Chucalissa Indian Museum; Danny and Virgie Solomon; and Jeffie Solomon, a grandmother who wove the beautiful basket that inspired the colors used in the drawings of the story.

Sam McCollum, a long-time farmer, taught me the ways of corn, including that to bring forth ears, it must grow in a group, a family. For centuries Native Americans have revered corn because it is a physical staple that, through the wisdom of its ways, also nourishes the spirit.

Pan Awsumb gave insightful criticism of the manuscript; Pat Cloar advised me on clothing of the period; and Paul Hicks, historian of First Methodist Church in Memphis, furnished many little-known facts and anecdotes. Dr. Charles Crawford of Memphis State University and Dr. Jim Roper of Southwestern University offered critical judgment and suggestions for reliable research sources on Memphis history. The staff of Memphis Public Library helped me carry through on the research, as did Steven Masler of the Museum of the River and Dr. Ronald Satz of the University of Tennessee at Martin.

Because of the nature of this story, I was fortunate to have Dr. Roger Easson, a distinguished Blake scholar, as my editor. He guided the writing with sensitivity and care. My husband, Paul, and our children— Alix, Audrey and Andrew—helped me in more ways than I can name. And the Grandmother came to me of her own accord. She is the one character I did not invent. She made her presence known. And when I asked, "Who are you?" she answered, "I am Ishtoua, the deliverer." For the mystery of her coming, I am profoundly grateful.

—Marilou Awiakta
Memphis, May 1983

For Paul
and our children
Alix, Audrey and Andrew

"**G**randmother, will we have to leave our home?"

"Your father comes back from the Council tonight, Rising Fawn. He will tell us."

It was the fourth night of the Cold Moon, the winter of Rising Fawn's seventh year. Her family had drawn their chairs around the cabin hearth, for chill air seeped through cracks in the shutters and narrow spaces between the floor planks.

Rising Fawn huddled on the Grandmother's lap. She took comfort in the familiar scent of the old woman, a clean, earthy scent mixed with the faint tang of warm pine. With that stout bosom at her back and the Grandmother's hands clasped across her chest like a clump of gnarled roots, Rising Fawn felt safe. She liked to feel the hands. Beneath their wrinkled brown skin, the flesh was still firm and strong close to the bone.

Ishtoua, the Grandmother. Ishtoua, the deliverer. Her wisdom would protect the family. And yet, she had not said they would be safe. Rising Fawn was afraid.

Her mother put aside the shirt she was sewing and got up to stir the fire, making the flames leap and crackle. Then she laid her hand on the wood chimney and ran her fingers along the grooves in the clay chinking.

"Your father's fingers made these grooves. When we married, the clan helped hew the logs and raise the cabin. But he smoothed every chink . . ."

Rising Fawn's brother, Kowichosh, had stopped reading his book and was studying his mother's face. Kowichosh, the bobcat. Quick-sighted. Quick-tempered. He was only twice Rising Fawn's age, but his face was already setting in the lines of a young warrior.

"They should not be allowed to take our land," he said. "They want it for more cotton fields, more money . . . In the three years since the Treaty of Dancing Rabbit Creek, they've taken almost everything that belonged to the Choctaw!"

His mother returned to her chair and took up the shirt, pushing the needle in and out of the blue wool she had carded, spun, and dyed herself. The daughter of Ishtoua was not easily pushed to anger or despair. "I can't believe our white neighbors would betray us. We speak their language. Our children play together. The chiefs and elders have listened to their missionaries with respect . . ."

"Mother, over six thousand Choctaw have already been removed. Hundreds have died on the march West. Why should the Government let *us* stay?"

"Perhaps they won't, Kowichosh." His mother paused in the middle of a stitch and looked at him firmly. "You are a good scholar at school. You understand many things. But you do not understand this . . . We can't give up hope until we know we must leave everything behind."

Abashed, Kowichosh turned back to his book, but Rising Fawn mulled the words, "leave everything behind . . . !" Leave school and friends . . . woods . . . fields of corn . . . the rock-rimmed pool in the creek where the family bathed every day, summer and winter . . . the cabin with its smell of wood fire, the crisp scent of drying meat and summer vegetables hanging from the rafters . . . the loft where she slept with the Grandmother on a mattress stuffed with corn shucks and pine boughs . . .

How the Grandmother loved pine! In the family cemetery, with its small wooden house over each grave, she had chosen a plot for herself beneath a large pine. Twice a year the family gathered for the cry ceremony to assure the spirits of the dead that their bones were cared for. And the Grandmother often said to Rising Fawn, "One day you will join the cry of the kindred for me. My spirit will hover near. I will be happy, as our ancestors have been when we remember them."

Rising Fawn nestled against the Grandmother. If they left everything behind, who would care for the bones of the family? Who would comfort their spirits? If the Grandmother should die, there would be no one left to remember. Rising Fawn wished her father would come. But the fire had burned low before they heard footsteps and the sound of the

latchstring. Everyone looked toward the door. Bending his head to miss the top of the door-jamb, her father came quietly into the room. Snow powdered his buckskin jacket and clung to strands of his hair. As he greeted them, his face was weary and sad. He put another log on the fire, warmed his hands before the new flames, then standing with his back to the hearth, he spoke slowly.

"The Council has debated for many days. Our clan chiefs and elders have decided—any of us who stay in Mississippi are a marked people. Already soldiers have burned some of our cabins to force us out. We must go to Indian Territory. We must leave our home."

The words passed through the family with the tremor of an earthquake and the ground beneath them seemed to shake and crack. They felt themselves falling into a bottomless dark.

For a time there was no sound except the steady sigh of the fire.

Rising Fawn clung to the Grandmother's hands. Kowichosh sat stiff and defiant. The Grandmother gazed steadily into the flames.

"How can we go?" asked the mother. "Our clan has many children and elders. The Big River is high and the current runs swift carrying many logs and branches. What does the Chief Headman say?"

"Chief Baha says our band will number almost a hundred. We will wait until the river goes down before we leave. Below Friar's Point, where Mulberry Island breaks the stream, the current is less swift. He has crossed safely there many times. The Government will not keep its promise to send boats and wagons, so we will have to build rafts and canoes. During the Moon of Wind we will cross. After that, we will walk."

"How long is the journey?"

"Four hundred miles."

Silence again. No one looked at the Grandmother. Such a distance was beyond her strength. She would surely die along the trail.

"Why don't our white neighbors help us?" Kowichosh asked. "The Choctaw have lived with them in peace. Our warriors fought with General Jackson against the British. Where are our white friends now?"

"They tell us they are sorry," the father said, "but it is the Government's doing and they cannot help us."

13

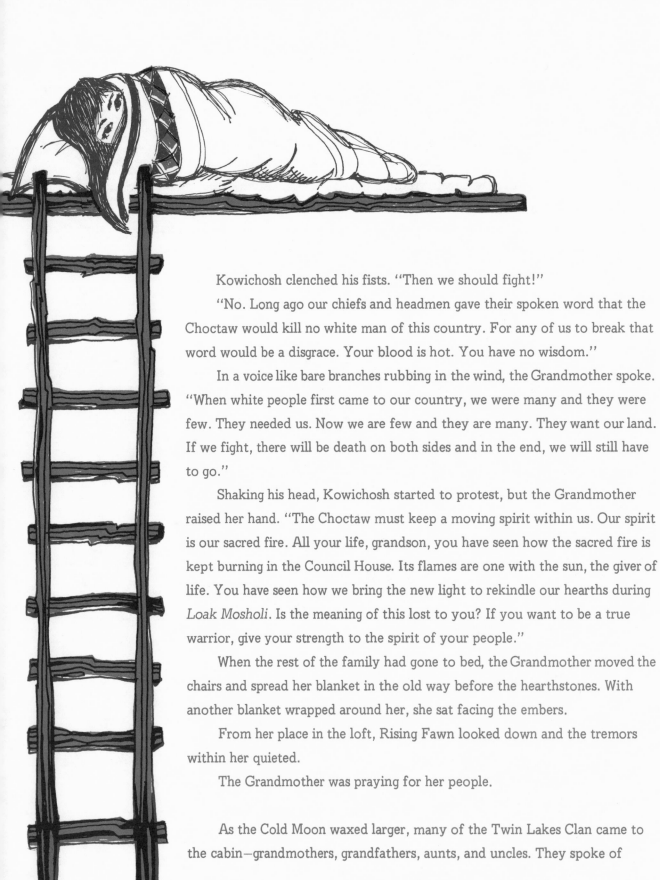

Kowichosh clenched his fists. "Then we should fight!"

"No. Long ago our chiefs and headmen gave their spoken word that the Choctaw would kill no white man of this country. For any of us to break that word would be a disgrace. Your blood is hot. You have no wisdom."

In a voice like bare branches rubbing in the wind, the Grandmother spoke. "When white people first came to our country, we were many and they were few. They needed us. Now we are few and they are many. They want our land. If we fight, there will be death on both sides and in the end, we will still have to go."

Shaking his head, Kowichosh started to protest, but the Grandmother raised her hand. "The Choctaw must keep a moving spirit within us. Our spirit is our sacred fire. All your life, grandson, you have seen how the sacred fire is kept burning in the Council House. Its flames are one with the sun, the giver of life. You have seen how we bring the new light to rekindle our hearths during *Loak Mosholi*. Is the meaning of this lost to you? If you want to be a true warrior, give your strength to the spirit of your people."

When the rest of the family had gone to bed, the Grandmother moved the chairs and spread her blanket in the old way before the hearthstones. With another blanket wrapped around her, she sat facing the embers.

From her place in the loft, Rising Fawn looked down and the tremors within her quieted.

The Grandmother was praying for her people.

As the Cold Moon waxed larger, many of the Twin Lakes Clan came to the cabin—grandmothers, grandfathers, aunts, and uncles. They spoke of sorrow and fear, of how to help each other. Most of all, they came to touch the wisdom of the Grandmother, who was the eldest.

Watching the family gather strength, Rising Fawn grew hopeful. But she went even more quietly than usual about her chores. Her mother smiled and said, "You are a child of your name—silent and quick. And those calm deer eyes miss nothing—you and your grandmother are alike in that. You two should choose the seed corn."

On one end of the worn plank table she heaped shucked ears. Some were deep orange. Others had gold kernels mingled with russet and soft black. "The chiefs and elders have given everyone a task for the journey and for making a home in the new land. We are to take choice seed corn for the fields. Your father and brother have brought deerskins for pouches. The fur will shed water and keep the seeds dry."

"And we must have seed enough for a large field," said the Grandmother. "The corn is like our people; it draws strength from its clan. A single stalk will bear nothing." How well the Grandmother knew the ways of corn. As she twisted an ear in her hands, kernels pattered onto the table so fast that Rising Fawn was kept busy scooping them into a willow basket. When it was full, she poured the kernels onto the table. They began to cull those too dark and hard to sprout.

From a pile of skins beside the fireplace, the mother took one, laid it on the floor and knelt to measure it. Rising Fawn peered over the edge of the table. "I want to carry seeds too. Will you make me a pouch?"

"I will make one small, like you, and put it on a

thong so you can wear it around your neck. You must
not lose it. It is a sacred task to carry seeds for the people,
for if the seeds are lost, the people will go hungry."

Rising Fawn was pleased and her curiosity quickened about
the new land. "In the West, Grandmother, will there be a new sky?
Will there be a Cup of Stars in the sky like we have here
to tell us when to plant the corn?"

Her question made the Grandmother chuckle.
"Of course, little one. Only land changes. The
sky will be the same. When the Cup of
Stars turns upside down like a dipper
spilling water, we will know that
Mother Earth is ready to receive
the seed. The Great Spirit has
made all things in harmony

and the wisdom of the Great Spirit is within each thing."

She pressed a round, russet kernel onto Rising Fawn's palm.

"Its heart is like a tiny flame of sacred fire. But feel how tough the shell is. You can throw the seed on the floor, put it in a pouch, carry it in your hand, but it will sprout only in warm earth. If it sprouts too soon, it will die. It protects itself until it is safe— that is its wisdom. The seed lives deep in its spirit until the time to come forth."

Closing Rising Fawn's hand around the kernel, she held the small fist in her root-like fingers. "The journey to the West will be hard. You will have to endure much. Be like the seed. Protect yourself. Live deep in your spirit until the time to come forth."

Rising Fawn turned this thought in her mind, then she asked, "How will I know when the time has come?"

"Listen to the wisdom within, where the Great Spirit speaks to you."

"Grandmother, when you pray before the fire, are you listening?"

"The fire is brother to the sun, the life giver. It helps me listen for the Great Spirit. When I pray I am listening . . . with my spirit-eyes and my spirit-ears."

Rising Fawn looked at the fire. "I see flames. I hear them snap and roar. That is all."

"You are using your body-eyes and body-ears," said the Grandmother. With her finger she tapped Rising Fawn's chest. "You must listen with your spirit-eyes and spirit-ears."

"Can you teach me how to listen?"

The Grandmother shook her head. "All I can teach you is to be still. You must ponder the fire mystery for yourself."

That night Rising Fawn tried hard to be still and pray with the Grandmother. She kept her eyes on the fire, but her mind circled the room. It touched the heavy deerskin pouches piled by the door . . . the loft where her brother was sleeping . . . the corner bed where her parents slept . . . the gourds filled with sugar and meal . . . the spinning wheel, her father's gun . . . baskets of berries, beans and squash . . . firelight dancing on her beaded moccasins . . . the snakeskin design glistening on her red dress . . . the small pouch, plump with seeds, around her neck . . . The Grandmother's eyes.

The eyes of the Grandmother were smiling, a smile that seemed to say, "To ponder a mystery takes patience. You are young. There is time."

Long after the Grandmother had gone to her bed in the loft, Rising Fawn lay on the blanket and gazed into the fire. She was warm and drifting to sleep when she felt a darkness gather about her, a faint tremor in the boards beneath her. Her first dazed thought was "Earthquake!" Then she realized horses were galloping close to the cabin. A shout brought her wide awake, a white man's shout . . .

"Burn it down! Gimme that torch. I'll throw it!"

Above the sound of hooves, another taut, urgent shout, "At least wake the family first, for god's sake!"

For answer, there was a thud against the cabin wall.

"Soldiers!" cried the father. He leapt from bed and climbed the loft ladder, "Wake up! Wake up!" Suddenly everyone else was moving—grabbing blankets, clothes, and as many pouches as they could carry. Rising Fawn stood by the hearth, holding her blanket around her. Through the cracks between the logs of the walls, smoke seeped into the room and she heard the warning of the flames.

Her mother thrust a heavy pouch into her hands. "Quick! Unbolt the door!"

She slid back the bolt, darted among the skittish horses. Startled, one horse reared above her. An arm jerked her out of the way, her dress sleeve tore . . .

the large pouch dropped. Hooves crashed down on it, seed corn scattered across the muddy snow. At the same time, she felt herself being drawn onto a

saddle and held tightly against a rough coat that smelled of
smoke and damp wool. She struggled and cried out, but the grim
faced soldier muttered, "At least I'll save one." Beneath the pounding feet of
the horse, the earth seemed once more to shake and crack. The crescent moon
swung back and forth in the sky. Rising Fawn felt herself falling into a darkness that became a dream. Her arms grew heavy, her eyelids heavier. She woke
once in a half daze. After a time, the pounding hooves gave way to a powerful
rocking and a sound of churning water. She dreamed the Big River flowed
cold around her. A cottonwood tree torn from its bank somewhere up river
swung heavily at her. She fought the wet branches—her fingers tore at the bark
She seemed caught in an endless cycle—rocking, rocking. She pulled her

blanket around her and pressed the deerskin pouch against her cheek. She tasted the salt of her tears.

In the sky, the Grandmother's hand tilted the Cup of Stars toward the earth. A voice like the embrace of wind in the pines whispered, "Be like the seed . . . live deep in your spirit . . ."

All motion stopped.

Rising Fawn opened her eyes.

She was in a box! Air and sunlight filtered through a crack in the lid, and she saw long scratches in the wood where she had tried to get out. Her fingers were raw and sore.

She heard a knocking . . .

A white man's voice shouted, "Christmas gift!"

A bolt sliding back. A door opening.

"Michael!" a woman cried " . . . come quick, James."

Another man's voice, this time heartier and older. "Welcome home, Michael. You're early. We didn't expect you in Memphis 'til Christmas Eve. Here, let me help you with that box." Rising Fawn felt a lifting, a carrying, a setting down. "I see you've marked it 'Clothes,' Michael. Mighty heavy for just clothes..."

"It isn't clothes," said the soldier. "It's something much more valuable. Something you and Amanda have wanted for a very long time . . ."

Light thumps of rope untying. Then the lid slowly sliding off.

In the bright light, the white faces blurred above her and Rising Fawn saw clearly only a grizzled beard, a yellow mustache and a coil of yellow braided hair. She clutched her deerskin pouch and felt tough kernels press against her palm. *"Be like the seed . . . Be like the seed."*

The woman bent closer. "It's a child, James . . . an Indian child!"

"Well, now . . ." The man with the grizzled beard laid his callosed hand on Rising Fawn's. Then he lifted her in his arms and went to sit in a chair beside the hearth.

Rising Fawn glanced furtively about the room—wood chimney, log walls, plank table, square bed in the corner. The cabin could be her own

home—except that the people were white, and strangers. Like a young doe trying to escape notice, she became very still. For a few moments the strangers were still also. Rising Fawn heard their soft breathing, the steady whisper of the fire . . . the flutter and cluck of chickens nesting under the floor.

From the box the woman brought the blanket and tucked it around the child. Kneeling beside the chair, she smoothed Rising Fawn's hair and touched her cheek. "She has beautiful eyes . . . so brown you can't see to the bottom." She looked at the torn dress, the fingers raw with scratches. "How did you come by this child, Michael?"

"Last night some men in my company got drunk and set on meanness. They knew about a Choctaw cabin in the woods near Friar's Point. They got it in their heads to burn it down. I tried to stop them. When I couldn't, I rode along to try to warn the family. I couldn't do that either. Things like this—and worse—happen all the time, Amanda. This removal is cruel work. I'm sick of it. When I saw that little girl run out of the burning cabin, something in me snapped. I grabbed her up and cut out . . . caught a steamboat at Friar's Point."

"What about her family?"

"Dead, maybe. If not, the cold will get them . . . or they'll die on the long walk West. I just said to myself, 'At least I'll save one.' And I did. Then I thought of you and James . . . 'Course, some folks hereabouts might say bad of you for taking an Indian girl for your own . . . If you don't want her, I guess I could . . ."

Rising Fawn looked up at the man holding her. His eyes were warm and brown. "Hmf," he said. "Somebody's always saying bad about something. If you're quality folks—or poor like us—nobody cares much what you do. Besides, after all these years clerking at Winchester's store, I've traded with an abundance of Chickasaws and Choctaws. I figure in the main, they're peaceable people—and honest. We'll love this little one and raise her for our own, won't we, Amanda? Now you can use that trundle bed you've been saving all this time."

The woman went to her brother and took both his hands. "The child will be a blessing to us. But you've brought trouble on yourself—you've deserted the Army, haven't you?"

The brother nodded. "I have. So I'm headed West. A man can disappear out there and get a new start."

"When will you go?"

"Right away. The Army is probably already on my trail, but they'll be asking about a soldier with an Indian child. Nobody saw me with her, because of the box. Your place may be where they'll look for me next. On the way from the Landing, I stopped by Anderson's Hotel. Found some folks passing through on their way to Texas. I'm going with them on the next ferry."

The woman put her arms around him. "You're the only one of my family left, Michael. I can't bear to think of you so far away . . . especially at Christmas . . . among strangers."

"Don't fret about me, Amanda. Think of that little girl. You and James are all she has now."

Rising Fawn felt the three of them looking at her but she fixed her eyes on the fire. The room, the faces, the things she had heard swirled in her mind and flowed away, except for the words, *"What about her family? Dead, maybe."* In the curling flames she saw the currents of the Big River and she knew, for her father had taught her, that in water all trails are lost. There was no way back to her family. No way for them to follow her, if any were alive to try.

Rising Fawn did not cry or speak . . . her silence became a tough shell as she withdrew deep in her spirit . . . to be like the seed and wait for the time to come forth . . . to listen for the Great Spirit . . .

From then on, only the fire was real to her. She thought of the white couple as simply "the Man" and "the Woman." With her body-ears and body-eyes she understood what they said, and she did as they asked, for they were Elders. But she never talked to them.

She turned her spirit to the fire. In the mornings she watched the Woman unbank the embers and stir them to life, then she helped the Man carry out ashes. When he brought in logs, she walked beside him, her arms heaped with branches and strips of bark, which she later fed, one by one, to the flames.

During the day, there were many chores to do—making butter and cottage cheese, spinning, weaving, plain sewing, beans to shell, meat to cook—but as she worked with the Woman, Rising Fawn

listened to the fire sing and crackle and sigh. She smelled the burning wood as it changed to warmth and light. At night, she sat on her blanket before the sandstone hearth, following the mysterious shift and leap of the flames. If she were very still, the spirit of the Grandmother came to sit beside her. But when Rising Fawn asked, *"Are you well? Is my family well?"* the Grandmother would not reply. The Great Spirit, too, was silent. And Rising Fawn knew she had not yet learned to be still enough.

"The child is *here,* but she isn't *with* us," the Woman told her husband. "I wonder if she'll ever truly be our own."

"She's likely grieving for her own people, Amanda. We'd best leave her be. We've got to be patient and gentle her slow." They began by forbidding her to bathe every day. "It'll weaken you," they said. "Once every week or two is enough." The smell of their bodies and of her own was much too ripe. But Rising Fawn paid it no mind.

The Woman made a dress for her. Using the torn red one for a pattern, she cut gray woolsey and sewed the seams by hand. No beads. No snakeskin design. Rising Fawn wore the dress, but she paid it no mind.

She was proud of her black hair, worn loose and shining in the way of the grandmothers. But while the Woman plaited it in two long braids, Rising Fawn stood without flinching. She paid them no mind.

The Man bought her a pair of high-topped shoes that laced up the front. The stiff leather hurt her ankles and the soles were so thick that when she went to the woodpile or to the spring, Rising Fawn couldn't feel the softness of Mother Earth beneath her feet, like she did in moccasins. She wore the shoes, but she paid them no mind.

"One last thing," said the Woman, "and you will almost look like one of us." She grasped the deerskin pouch to take it off. Rising Fawn took her hand and gently pulled it away.

Stepping back, the Woman looked at her a long time, then shook her head sadly. Rising Fawn went to sit before the fire. She murmured to herself in Choctaw, "It is hard to be like the seed . . ."

Later, when she thought Rising Fawn was asleep, the Woman said in a low voice, "The child understands what we say, James. I'm sure she could speak, if she would. There's

a knowing in her eyes—and something else. Sometimes they seem like the eyes of an old woman, wise and distant. I think she has a pagan soul."

"Amanda, maybe it's just the difference you're seeing. You're used to white children."

"No. No. From the day she came I've been watching her. She prays to the fire, worships it. I know that pouch is a heathen thing. Tomorrow we must take her to church. With Christmas so near, I'm sure Brother Owen will tell the story of the Christ Child. It will do her soul good to hear it."

The Man sighed. "Hearing is one thing. Accepting is another. Indians call God the 'Great Spirit,' and they have different ways of worshiping Him. You can change an Indian on the outside, but deep down, he'll keep to his own ways."

"That may be. But it can't do anybody harm to be in God's House."

Rising Fawn was listening. "Pagan" and "heathen" were unknown words to her, but they had a bad sound. She put them from her mind and puzzled over other words that sounded good—"Christmas," "Christ Child," "God's House." Sometimes she'd heard white children use the words, but Rising Fawn had never before been curious about what they meant. Maybe God's House was like the Choctaws' Council House. Maybe she would feel at home there.

The next morning the Woman pinned a white collar on her black poplin dress and tucked the pouch under the bodice of Rising Fawn's gray one. "We don't wear ornaments in God's House," she said. "It's irreverent. You shouldn't wear that heathen pouch at all."

Inwardly, Rising Fawn smiled, because the pouch made a funny gray bump on her chest. "White people are strange," she thought. "Christmas must be one of their great ceremonies, with prayers and sacred dances and a feast. But they don't prepare for it. No bright clothes. No bead and feather symbols. Nothing to celebrate and honor the Great Spirit. Surely, though, they will have a sacred fire in their Council House . . ."

She looked forward to hearing about the Christ Child. When the clan elders told an important story, the Grandmother always said, "In the telling is a wisdom for the people." And Rising Fawn was glad the Christmas story was about a child, like herself.

These things flickered in her mind as they set out in the wagon. She sat in the back, jostling with each lurch and bump. "It's a good thing we have clear skies," the Man said.

"Rain in Memphis means
mud to your knees and some of these holes
are deep enough to drown an ox."

Rising Fawn was thinking of the thick
woods on either side of the road. Branches
swayed and rubbed together in the wind, like the
voice of the Grandmother, speaking without words. The
sound quieted her spirit and made her more aware of what was happening
around her.

They turned into a wider road, with stumps newly cut just low enough
to let the wagon axle pass. Once in a while the wheels would slip in a rut
and bang the wagon bed on a stump. A bell was clanging in the distance.

"This is Poplar Street," the Man said over his shoulder. "Yonder in the field on
Second—that little white, frame building—that's the Methodist Meeting House. We built
it last year. It's the only church in Memphis. Started with eleven members and now we
have about fifty."

"And we have our own bell too," the Woman added. "It's up on a pole and the preacher
shakes the pole to ring it. Before that we had to use the hotel bell to call the people."

They sounded pleased and proud. As the wagon pulled up among high weeds in the
churchyard, Rising Fawn saw many people gathering. Some came on foot. Some came on
horseback. God's House surprised her. It was four-cornered, like the Council House, but
instead of one door in front, there were two. Women were going in by the left door, men by
the right. Inside, it was quiet and smelled of new wood. The walls were smooth, and white.
Sunlight streamed brightly through the clear glass windows. There was one aisle between two
rows of benches made of planks laid loose on blocks, some high, some low.

Rising Fawn sat with the Woman on the left side. She wondered why everyone faced

forward. Without a circle, how would the chiefs and elders see each other when they spoke? And why did the people wear such drab, dull colors? Rising Fawn was glad to see many dark faces among the white. Some were black and shining, like sun on a raven's wing. Others were warm brown shades of Mother Earth. Beside her a slim woman with skin almost like her own smiled at her.

Rising Fawn smiled back.

But she was disturbed. Nowhere was there a sacred fire. And the ceremony seemed odd. Someone struck a tuning fork and the people sang. Rising Fawn caught one phrase "how sweet the sound . . ." The sound was sweet, but there was no drum, no steady, dancing beat. Perhaps the dances would come later.

Oddest of all, when the people prayed, they bowed their heads and closed their eyes. How could they hear the Great Spirit if they turned their faces away, if they didn't listen with their eyes as well as their ears . . . ?

After the prayer, the Woman whispered, "Brother Owen will preach now. You'll like him. Sometimes he soars aloft and takes us into the third heaven."

Rising Fawn made no sense of these words, except that Brother Owen must be a chief who had the power of an eagle. Quietly, he began the story of the Christ Child and the great star that foretold his birth. At the word, "star," Rising Fawn leaned forward to listen better.

Then the Chief began to speak of a "king mighty in his wickedness" and of "Light overcoming Darkness." He uttered strange words like "sin" and "redemption." Rising Fawn lost the thread of the story. She began to listen, not to the words, but to their rhythm, that rose and fell and rose again. The Chief did not pause for any Elders to speak, but went on and on. As he talked he waved his arms. The waving became faster as his voice rose louder and higher—up, up, up. Rising Fawn expected him to mount into the air.

Instead, a bench gave way and five people fell to the floor.

There was more singing. Brother Owen raised his hand for a prayer. And the ceremony was over.

Outside again, people seemed satisfied and happy. They greeted each other and some called out, "Merry Christmas," as they parted.

Bumping along the road in the wagon, Rising Fawn was glad when the churchyard ended and the trees began again. She listened to the wind flow from tree to tree, moving along beside her, and she whispered in Choctaw, "Grandmother . . . these people are strange beyond all knowing. Their spirit has no sacred fire. Their ceremony has no dance. And they leave the Christ Child with his story half-told. How can anyone learn its wisdom if the story is half-told?"

The stirring of the branches reminded her, "Live deep in your spirit. Be still . . . listen . . ." But when the wagon crossed a street edged with log houses, Rising Fawn entered a boisterous world that sent her spirit skittering like corn across a stone floor.

"Market Square—the center of town," announced the Man. He stopped the wagon by a hard-packed plot dotted with tall trees. Around the square were low buildings, made of boards or hewn logs. The Man pointed out several stores, the courthouse and the jail, saying, "They bring the prisoners across the street there to Anderson's Hotel for meals . . . guess they figure a hungry man won't bolt! Next to the jail is . . ."

But Rising Fawn was too startled to pay attention. Hogs were rooting in heaps of garbage that had been thrown into the street. The door of one of the cabins opened and a woman emptied a chamber pot near the doorstep. The Grandmother always said, "No self-respecting animal—or person—fouls its own nest." But the smell and look of the square was certainly foul!

Two women were walking across the square. One wore a fire-red dress and a hat with red and pink feathers. The other was dressed all in purple. Although their faces were painted, and their clothes bright, Rising Fawn was sure they were not headed for a ceremony. Perhaps it was because of the way they stopped to laugh and talk with the men. Most of the people in the square were men. Some wore buckskins and were riding horses—they were most likely trappers. Others stomped along in boots and denims, talking loudly and making jokes.

A mule pulling a small farm wagon stepped in a deep hole in the road and could not get out. No matter how hard the farmer swore and pulled on the bridle, the mule could not be budged. The farmer unhitched the wagon, pulled it off to the side of the road and went into a saloon, leaving the mule to save himself.

The Woman shook her head and said to Rising Fawn, "Now you see why respectable womenfolk never come to town alone. Between flatboatmen, Indians and, yes, men from hereabouts drinking and acting like heathens, the streets aren't safe."

"Don't forget the bears, Amanda," the Man said wryly. "Sometimes they wander in from the woods, not to mention the panthers and pole cats."

"Hmf! I'd rather face any one of them than some of these men. What Mayor Rawlings ought to do is close down the saloons and build more churches. Whiskey leads to dancing you know."

"Amanda, you're forgetting that the Methodists used to meet in the Blue Ruin Tavern before they built the church."

"We just met in the dining room, not the bar," she answered sharply.

To Rising Fawn the connections the Woman made between "dancing," "heathens," "whiskey," and "church" were confusing. The elders had always been stern about whiskey. It was forbidden. That much, at least, she understood. The men she saw made her nervous because most of them were bearded, and Choctaw men never were. Oddly, apart from the first moment she saw him, she had never been frightened of the Woman's husband. In fact, she hardly noticed his beard any more. Perhaps it was because he was so kindly.

As he clucked to the horse and the wagon moved around the corner to Main Street, he said over his shoulder, "Guess all this noise is a little upsetting to you, child. But Memphis is just now sprouting into a town. We're getting civilized. We have a newspaper called the *Advocate*, and a town council. Sometimes Sol Smith brings his players down from Cincinnati. We'll have to take you to see Mr. and Mrs. Marks in 'The Day After the Fair,' or 'The Lover's Quarrel.' I expect we can get Sister Ann Kesterson to come from the church to teach you your letters. If you were a boy—and we had some money or some land to trade for the teaching—you could go to the Irishman, Mr. Magevney. He keeps school in a cabin near our place. There's plans to make a square there too—'Court Square' I think they call it. So far the square's no more than a few stakes in the woods, but it'll get cleared by and by."

Rising Fawn was only half-listening. Among the stores and houses on Main Street were many trees and she watched them as much as she could, trying to keep in touch with the voice of the Grandmother. But when the wagon turned into a narrow alley, she saw only a few scraggly bushes, some old papers, meat bones, a soggy feather mattress, and a dead dog among the buildings.

"Now this shackledy place," said the Man stopping the wagon, "is all that's left of the Bell Tavern—just enough left standing for a bar. Last winter some poor folks got mighty cold. Ole Judge Overton over in Nashville owns a lot of forest property around here, but he wouldn't let a soul get any firewood from it. So some folks came and chopped up all the Tavern's sleeping rooms for firewood. Then hogs got into it, rooting and knocking the boards loose and that's all that's left."

It sounded as if the hogs were still in it. Rising Fawn heard grunts, shouts, thumps, and shattering glass. Pulling the wagon to the side of the alley, the Man said, "A big fight's going on in there. Wait a bit and you'll see a sight. Hear that clatter and shouting off in the distance? They're bringing up our fire engine, Little Vigor."

Eight men soon came running down the alley, pulling a bell-shaped pump about three feet high. Other men, curious and eager, ran alongside.

The Woman looked alarmed. "Move on, James. They're liable to get in a big way and douse us too!"

"Now, Amanda, we don't want to miss the fun. We'll be all right."

When the engine was in place, six men began to pump the cranks. While one man held open the Tavern door, another aimed the hose at the opening. Such a foul-smelling stream of water rushed out that Rising Fawn held her nose.

The Man chuckled. "They've filled her up again at the hog wallow down at Auction Square." Suddenly, men burst out of the tavern, swearing, staggering, holding their arms in front of their faces as they ran in all directions.

The wagon moved on too. "Yes sir, be it a fight or a fire, Little Vigor can take care of it. She can throw a stream over the highest house in town . . . which I'm going to show to

you directly. It's right around here where Chickasaw runs into Mississippi Row. By the way, there's the Blue Ruin. They call it that because they say when folks drink a lot of gin there, it turns their skin blue!''

The building was painted bright blue too. Rising Fawn liked the color, but the Woman said, "James, you do beat all. What's the child going to think of us!"

Soon they came to a two-story frame house, set in a grove of bare-limbed locust trees. Slowing the wagon the Man said, "This is Major Winchester's—and that's his store there beside it, where I work."

Racoon and deer hides were tacked to the wall and goods lined the porch of the store— sacks of corn, piles of skins, a heavy bedstead, a plow—and there was a sign nailed to a post which the Man told Rising Fawn said, "Clothes—Blue, Black and Fancy." A tall Indian was examining the bedstead. From his belted chintz tunic and the turban on his head, Rising Fawn knew he was Chickasaw. She felt a sharp loneliness for her own people and a yearning to be at home again. "Major Winchester," the Man went on, "is one of the quality folks in Memphis. Was our first mayor. Now he's the Postmaster and Land Agent. This is the only two-story house in Memphis . . . even has a ballroom on the second floor."

The Woman frowned. "Dancing leads to all manner of wickedness! That's why Josiah Baker was thrown out of church last year. Somebody caught him looking in the hotel ballroom and tapping his foot. Dancing is a heathen practice. No child of mine will ever have any part of it."

Brisk and impatient, the wind rattled the branches of the locust trees and Rising Fawn murmured, "Did you hear what she said, Grandmother? 'Dancing leads to wicked-ness.' How can sacred dancing be wicked? I will never understand these people. I don't want to be in their noisy, confusing world."

As the wagon rolled along the promenade, Rising Fawn looked out over the bluff.

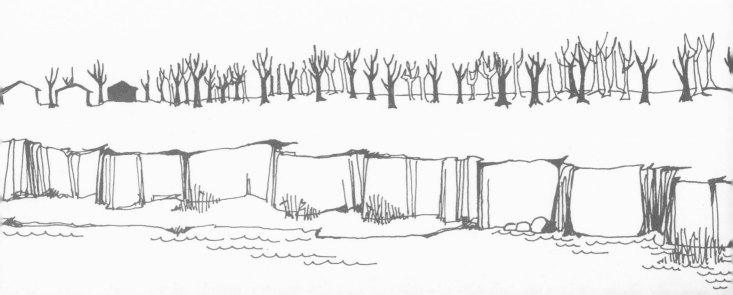

Beyond the expanse of tall grass and blackberry brambles, the Big River stretched wide and swift—the great, muddy waters where all trails are lost. Memories of the burning cabin and the night of endless rocking flowed around her. She began to shake and her heart cried out, "Grandmother . . . Grandmother . . ."

Having no trees to give it voice, the Grandmother's spirit swept away down the river.

Rising Fawn lay down on her side in the wagon bed, with her legs drawn up, curling her head to her knees. When she heard the Woman ask what was the matter, she did not even look up. And when they were at the cabin again, Rising Fawn withdrew even deeper into her kernel of silence.

That night the spirit of the Grandmother did not come to sit by the hearth. Nor did she come the next night, or the next. To Rising Fawn the mystery of the fire was hidden more than ever. Why had the Grandmother left her alone? Why did the Great Spirit not speak? Would there ever be a time to come forth or would the flame of her spirit go out and leave her useless, like a culled seed? The wondering was so great that she became more and more still. And the Man and Woman rarely talked, even to each other.

Because there were no words to distract her, Rising Fawn began to listen with her spirit-eyes and spirit-ears. Gradually she began to see the fire not only as a cherished link with home and family, but as a living presence with a spirit of its own. Sitting within the circle of its warm and shifting light, she felt the tough thick shell around her soften and grow more thin.

For the first time she noticed that the Woman's eyes were hazel and sad with yearning. She remembered her bending over the gray woolsey, sewing seams with careful stitches, remembered her saying to the Man, "I wonder if the child will ever truly be our own?"

And the Man had said, "She's likely grieving for her own people. Leave her be." He understood so much. And he had been the first to say, "We'll love her and raise her for our own." Now he seemed distant and his step was slower, older.

Rising Fawn sensed the Man and Woman were thinking about her too. Out of the corners of her eyes, she often saw them watch her, then look a long time at each other. Once the Woman bowed her head, as if to hide tears, and the Man touched her gently on the cheek.

Rising Fawn had never realized before how alone they were. No one from their clan ever came to comfort and cheer them. She had listened to them only with her body-eyes and body-ears. And it was not enough.

The Grandmother had once said, "All I can teach you is to be still." Rising Fawn murmured, "I have learned, Grandmother. You have taught me by your coming—and by your going—how to be still. Come back and show me the mystery of the fire . . ."

One morning, when the sun was high, Rising Fawn woke to a new stir in the cabin and the smell of frying sidemeat. The Woman was at the hearth, tending iron pots that sat among the coals or hung on hooks above the fire. Over her homespun dress she wore a fresh white apron, and over her hair a muslin cap that tied under her chin.

Rising Fawn heard her say, "Get up child, and rejoice. It's Christmas! The neighbors will be soon firing their guns to celebrate. You couldn't sleep through that racket anyway. If James were home, he'd be shooting his gun to join in the fun."

Christmas! Rising Fawn blinked. She'd thought the ceremony at the church was Christmas.

"Hurry along now—it's the birthday of the Christ Child. Come and help me get ready."

Rising Fawn eased out of her trundle bed and went to the hearth. Although she didn't speak, she was smiling. If it were the Christ Child's birthday, she thought, perhaps someone would tell the rest of his story. And there was to be a feast after all. As the Woman lifted the lid of each pot, Rising Fawn leaned to smell the steam: peas, greens, potatoes, sweet apples with dumplings—and a guinea hen roasting on the spit.

"James will be home from the store by dusk," the Woman said. "We have a sight of chores to do. I haven't even gotten out my mother's linen cloth for the table yet. I brought it all the way from Mecklenburg, North Carolina, and that's been most ten years ago . . . we'll use the blue crockery plates too, instead of the pewter ones. Hurry now and get dressed."

The plank floor was cold to her feet so that Rising Fawn trotted across it quickly, smiling at the quarrelsome cluck of the hens who didn't like such sharp sounds above them. She came to the peg on the wall where she'd hung her clothes . . . and stopped. On the peg was her red dress—freshly washed, pieced, and mended neatly at the shoulder with a scrap of woolsey. On the floor were her moccasins, set side by side.

She looked back. The Woman had turned again to her cooking. Putting on the dress and moccasins, Rising Fawn went to stand beside her, shy with pleasure. The Woman looked down at her. "Mind you, it's just for today, just for Christmas." But her voice had a cheerful lilt. "Come now, we have work to do."

Rising Fawn enjoyed helping her. While the Woman held up one of the floor planks, Rising Fawn shooed two hens from their nests and gathered the warm, brown eggs. With a pine branch she swept the floor, pushing the dust into the narrow cracks between the planks onto the earth beneath. The constant swishing warmed the pine and in the tang of it, Rising Fawn smelled the familiar, comforting scent of the Grandmother.

"When you've finished sweeping child, come help me make the cornbread," the Woman said. On the plank table the Woman put a bowl of shucked corn that had been soaked in water. Rising Fawn dried each cob with a cloth. Into another bowl the Woman put a piece of tin punctured with nail holes. As she scraped a cob against the rough side, coarse meal sifted through. Rising Fawn watched it mounding, and picked out random kernels that popped off whole. She licked the sweet meal off one, then held the kernel in her palm. It was different from Indian corn—white, large, and rather flat, with one end tapering. But in the center she saw its heart, pale ivory and shaped like a flame. She closed her hand around it. "It is a sacred task to carry seeds for the people," her mother had said. But Rising Fawn knew her people would go to the new land without her. Her seeds would never be planted there. And though she had tried to be still and listen to the wisdom within, as the Grandmother had taught her, the Great Spirit had not spoken. It was not yet time to come forth.

The Woman had stopped stirring the cornbread. Looking up, Rising Fawn saw that she was watching her, with an expression curious and tender. "Child, can you show me now . . . what is in the pouch?"

Slowly, Rising Fawn opened her hand. The Woman touched the kernel, then the pouch. "Do you mean to tell me, it's filled with seed corn? Just seed corn?" When Rising Fawn nodded, the Woman smiled, as if she were bewildered and at the same time immensely relieved.

At dusk, when the Man's wagon rumbled into the clearing, Rising Fawn opened the door for him. The air was cold, the wind quiet. Beyond the web of branches in the woods, a full moon was rising. The Man walked slowly toward the door. "Well, now . . . it's mighty heartening to have you greet me. I see you're wearing your Indian dress—red is a good

present for a brown-eyed girl. I've brought you a present too . . . for after supper." When the dishes had been done and the cloth folded away, Rising Fawn sat on her blanket by the hearth, facing the Man and Woman, who had drawn their chairs, side by side, within the circle of firelight.

"Christmas Gift!" From his pocket, the Man drew out two things Rising Fawn had never seen before. One was shaped like a harvest moon, small, the color of pumpkins. "This is an orange," he said, "and this . . . is a stick of peppermint candy. When you're ready to eat them, I'll show you how to cut a hole in the orange and suck the juice up through the peppermint."

Rising Fawn took the gifts. She smelled the orange, then tasted the candy, following the red stripes with the tip of her tongue. She wanted to save the treats . . . make them last as long as possible. She wished she had something to give the Man and the Woman. The Woman must have sensed her wish, for she said, "Child, we want to love you and raise you for our own. If you want to give us a gift, speak to us. Tell us your name—just your name. That would be a beginning . . ."

When Rising Fawn drew back, the Woman patted her hand. "Never mind. I know you'll speak to us some day, in your own good time . . . For now, why don't you help me fix the Christmas candle in the window? We put it there for the Christ Child. Do you remember his story? Brother Owen told it at church.

Rising Fawn shook her head. All she remembered was that a great star appeared in the sky to show the people that the Christ Child had come to earth. But Brother Owen had left the story half-told. "The Great Spirit has made all things in harmony and the wisdom of the Great Spirit is within each thing," so said the Grandmother. But who could find the wisdom in half a story? Rising Fawn was eager to hear all of it, and she smiled at the Woman to let her know.

"She's forgotten the story, James. But she wants to hear it again. Why don't you tell her . . . you know how to talk to her better than I do."

The Man rubbed his beard, then leaned forward with his elbows resting on his knees. "I don't know my letters, so I can't read it to you from the Bible. I'll just have to tell it to you plain."

"As you have cause enough to know, some people are set on being mean. But God . . . the Great Spirit . . . wants all his people to love each other and live in peace. So, he sent his son to show us how to do it. But he sent him as a little child . . . like a little candle in the dark, so to speak. And he sent him to a family—a man and a woman—because a child can't hardly make it in this world without a family. The Christ Child came down to earth at Christmas . . ."

"And that's why we put a candle in the window," the Woman said, "so when the Christ Child's spirit passes, he will see it and know he is welcome. It's a way of inviting love to come in."

"Sometimes he comes in the form of his own spirit," the Man went on. "And sometimes he comes in the form of a stranger . . . maybe like you've come to us . . ."

Rising Fawn had been listening intently, with the seed pouch pressed against her cheek. She felt the wisdom in the story, but a clear understanding was slow to come. She was still mulling over it as she put the tallow candle in its pewter holder and set it on the window sill. The Woman lit a twig at the fire and brought it to the window. "Here child . . . you light the candle . . ."

As Rising Fawn touched the burning twig to the wick, she thought of the Christ Child . . . of her own wandering . . . of her own hearth where the fire was kindled every year from the source of all life . . .

When the Woman moved back to her seat at the hearth, Rising Fawn barely heard the rustle of skirts . . . the creak of the chair . . . the candle flame was drawing her spirit-eyes and spirit-ears into its tiny light . . . and beyond, for the window pane seemed to cast its reflection outside where it flickered like a seed of fire in the lap of night.

When the Man stirred the embering logs, the window also reflected the leaping flames.

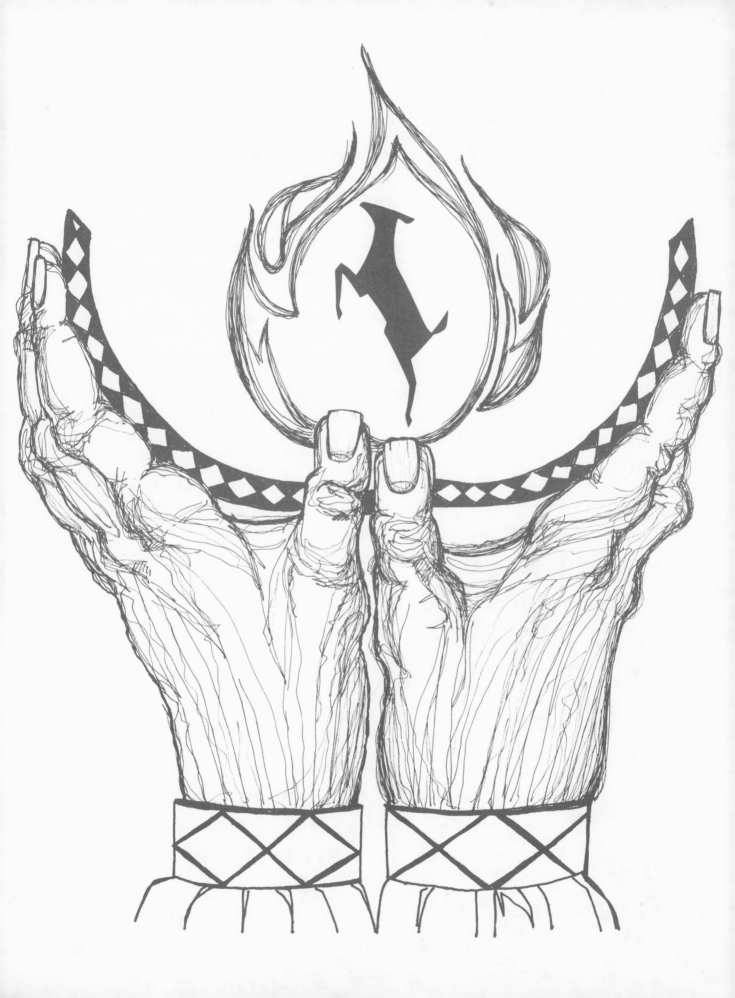

Rising Fawn watched them blaze brighter and larger around the candle's light. Many flames, one fire. Like the life of the seed caught in the shell of the corn, she stood watching the fire within the fire, and she felt its light kindled within her. Ablaze with recognition, she knew this was like *Loak Mosholi*, when each family in the clan kindled its cabin fire with a burning brand carried from the sacred fire in the Council House. Each family was the flame within the flame. In a way she could not quite explain, she understood that she herself contained a tiny flame from which the clan would draw its own strength. It was a flame which flowed from the source of all fires and at the same time from the source of all waters.

As her gaze deepened, she saw the smaller flame move in a silence so deep that she felt the wisdom within rise and the Great Spirit began to speak—not in words but in images. She dared not move, and her body-ears told Rising Fawn a patient and loving silence had fallen upon the room behind her.

From the heart of the candle flame Rising Fawn saw the Grandmother's gnarled hands slowly unfold and spread like a wide cup to hold the sacred flame.

She saw the faces of the Man and the Woman and felt their love flow through the Grandmother's fingers into the firelight around her, warm as the earth.

She saw a russet kernel of corn. Its tough shell began to part as the slender sprout pushed upward—unfolding a tiny gleaming leaf—and downward, stretching a tendril root toward the earth.

She understood that her spirit was safe. She understood also that she too would always carry seeds for her people, but that her seeds would come forth in this new land.

Quietly, she felt a new confidence, and a deep relief that there was to be a time for her to come forth like the flame within the seed had come forth. She turned around and moved close to the Man and the Woman who had been watching her. They sat still, expectant. Rising Fawn folded one small hand around the Man's rough knuckles, and the other she placed within the up-turned palm of the Woman. With a soft voice she said,

"My name is Rising Fawn."

ABOUT THE AUTHOR

Marilou (Thompson) Awiakta, a widely published Cherokee/Appalachian poet and lecturer, has been active for most of her professional life in Native American issues. Her first book, *Abiding Appalachia: Where Mountain and Atom Meet,* is in its fourth printing with St. Luke's. *Rising Fawn* is her first book for children. A Tennessean, Awiakta grew up in Oak Ridge and received her BA degree from the University of Tennessee.

ABOUT THE ILLUSTRATOR

Beverly Bringle, a native of Covington, Tennessee, is of Choctaw descent, her great-grandfather, as a child, having endured the infamy of removal along the Trail of Tears. She holds the MFA degree from the University of Guanajuato and presently teaches art in the Stoneham Public Schools in the greater Boston area. She has exhibited both in Mexico and this country.

A Series of Books for Christmas from St. Luke's Press